THIS WALKER BOOK
BELONGS TO:

· · · · · · · · · · · · · · ·

· · · · · · · · · · · · · · ·

· · · · · · · · · · · · · · ·

For Will and Justin

First published 2011 by Walker Books Ltd
87 Vauxhall Walk, London SE11 5HJ

This edition published 2012

20 19 18 17 16 15 14 13 12

© 2011 Jon Klassen

The right of Jon Klassen to be identified as author/illustrator
of this work has been asserted by him in accordance with
the Copyright, Designs and Patents Act 1988

This book has been typeset in New Century Schoolbook

Printed in China

British Library Cataloguing in Publication Data:
a catalogue record for this book is available from the British Library

ISBN 978-1-4063-3853-9

www.walker.co.uk

I
WANT
MY
HAT
BACK

JON KLASSEN

WALKER BOOKS
AND SUBSIDIARIES
LONDON • BOSTON • SYDNEY • AUCKLAND

My hat is gone.
I want it back.

Have you seen my hat?

No. I haven't seen your hat.

OK. Thank you anyway.

Have you seen my hat?

No. I have not seen any hats around here.

OK. Thank you anyway.

Have you seen my hat?

No. Why are you asking me.
I haven't seen it.
I haven't seen any hats anywhere.
I would not steal a hat.
Don't ask me any more questions.

OK. Thank you anyway.

Have you seen my hat?

I haven't seen anything all day. I have been trying to climb this rock.

Would you like me to lift you on top of it?

Yes, please.

Have you seen my hat?

I saw a hat once.
It was blue and round.

My hat doesn't look like that.
Thank you anyway.

Have you seen my hat?

What is a hat?

Thank you anyway.

Nobody has seen my hat.
What if I never see it again?
What if nobody ever finds it?

My poor hat.
I miss it so much.

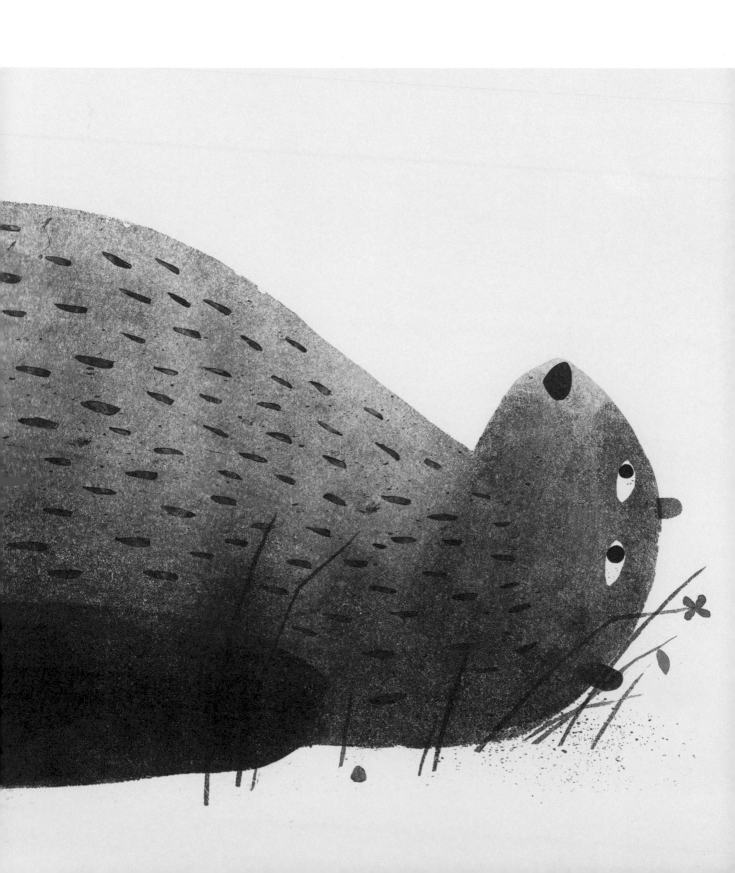

What's the matter?

I have lost my hat.
And nobody has seen it.

What does your hat look like?

It is red and pointy and . . .

I HAVE
SEEN MY HAT.

YOU. YOU STOLE MY HAT.

I love my hat.

Excuse me, have you seen
a rabbit wearing a hat?

No. Why are you asking me.
I haven't seen him.
I haven't seen any rabbits
anywhere.
I would not eat a rabbit.
Don't ask me any more questions.

OK. Thank you anyway.

JON KLASSEN is the author-illustrator of *We Found a Hat* and *This Is Not My Hat*, the only book to ever win both the Kate Greenaway and Caldecott Medal. He also illustrated *Extra Yarn* and the Caldecott Honor book *Sam and Dave Dig a Hole*, both written by Mac Barnett, as well as Ted Kooser's *House Held Up by Trees*. Before making picture books, he served as an illustrator on the animated feature film, *Coraline*. Originally from Niagara Falls, Canada, Jon now lives in Los Angeles, USA with his wife.

Find Jon online at www.burstofbeaden.com, on Twitter as @burstofbeaden and on Instagram as @jonklassen.

Photo credit Autumn Le' Brannon

www.walker.co.uk